HENRY
THE BULL
AND HIS FRIENDS

HEMA RISHI SHARMA

NewDelhi • London

BLUEROSE PUBLISHERS
India | U.K.

Copyright © Hema Rishi Sharma 2025

All rights reserved by author. No part of this publication may be reproduced, stored in a retrieval system or transmitted in any form or by any means, electronic, mechanical, photocopying, recording or otherwise, without the prior permission of the author. Although every precaution has been taken to verify the accuracy of the information contained herein, the publisher assume no responsibility for any errors or omissions. No liability is assumed for damages that may result from the use of information contained within.

BlueRose Publishers takes no responsibility for any damages, losses, or liabilities that may arise from the use or misuse of the information, products, or services provided in this publication.

For permissions requests or inquiries regarding this publication, please contact:

BLUEROSE PUBLISHERS
www.BlueRoseONE.com
info@bluerosepublishers.com
+91 8882 898 898
+4407342408967

ISBN: 978-93-6783-734-4

Cover design: Yash Singhal
Typesetting: Namrata Saini

First Edition: May 2025

Contents

Chapter 1: The Meadow 1
Chapter 2: A Change Begins 3
Chapter 3: The First Act of Kindness .. 5
Chapter 4: A Stormy Challenge 7
Chapter 5: A Test of Forgiveness 9
Chapter 6: Earning Trust 11
Chapter 7: The Surprise Picnic 13
Chapter 8: Happily Ever After 15

Chapter 2: A Change Begins

But one day, everything changed. A wise old owl named Oliver flew down and perched on a tree branch near Henry. "Why do you always scare everyone, Henry?" Oliver asked. "You could have so many friends if you were kinder."

Henry snorted. "Friends? Who needs them? I'm strong enough on my own!"

Oliver shook his head. "Strength isn't just about muscles, Henry. It's about the heart too."

That night, Henry couldn't sleep. He thought about what Oliver had said. "Maybe I should try being nicer," he mumbled to himself.

Chapter 3: The First Act of Kindness

The next morning, Henry decided to change. He saw Rosie struggling to reach a tasty-looking apple hanging from a tree. Instead of scaring her, Henry gently used his strong horns to knock the apple down. "Here you go, Rosie," he said with a smile.

Rosie looked surprised but smiled back. "Thank you, Henry!" she said, nibbling on the apple.

Chapter 4: A Stormy Challenge

A few days after Henry's first act of kindness, a big storm hit the meadow. The wind howled, and rain poured down, flooding the animals' homes. Henry noticed that Rosie's burrow was filling with water, and she was shivering on top of a rock, unable to escape the rising water.

Without hesitation, Henry charged through the rain, using his strong horns to lift Rosie onto his back. He carried her to a nearby tree, where it was safe and dry. "Thank you, Henry!" Rosie said, her eyes wide with gratitude.

Henry smiled. "Friends help each other," he replied, feeling warmth spread through him despite the cold rain.

As the storm raged on, Henry continued to help other animals, guiding them to safety. When the storm finally passed, the animals huddled together, grateful for Henry's bravery. They realized that his strength was not just in his muscles but in his heart.

Chapter 5:
A Test of Forgiveness

One morning, as the sun shone brightly again, a large group of deer came to the meadow. They were strong, just like Henry, but they had a habit of pushing others around. Henry watched as they bullied the smaller animals, just like he used to do.

Feeling a pang of guilt, Henry approached the biggest deer, who was laughing at Rosie. "That's not how we treat friends here," Henry said firmly.

The deer sneered. "And who are you to tell us what to do?"

"I used to be like you," Henry replied calmly. "But I learned that being strong doesn't mean hurting others. It means helping them."

The deer paused, then snorted and walked away. Henry turned back to Rosie, who was looking up at him with wide eyes. "You've really changed, Henry," she said.

"Thanks to you and everyone else," Henry said, feeling his heart swell with pride. He knew that he would never go back to being the old Henry, and that made him happier than anything else.

Chapter 6: Earning Trust

Word quickly spread through the meadow about Henry's change of heart. The other animals were curious but still a bit wary. Later that day, Henry saw Timmy the Turtle stuck on his back, unable to flip over. Henry carefully nudged Timmy with his nose until he was right side up.

"Thanks, Henry!" Timmy said, crawling happily away.

Slowly but surely, Henry's kind actions started to make a difference. The animals began to trust him, and Henry found himself laughing and playing with them. He realized that having friends made the meadow a much happier place.

Chapter 7: The Surprise Picnic

One afternoon, the animals decided to throw a surprise picnic for Henry. As he approached the big oak tree, he saw all his new friends gathered with food and games.

"For being such a good friend, Henry!" they all cheered.

Henry's heart swelled with joy. "Thank you, everyone! I'm so happy to have friends like you."

Chapter 8: Happily Ever After

From that day on, Henry the Bull was known as the friendliest animal in the meadow, and he never felt lonely again. He learned that being kind and helping others made him feel stronger and happier than ever before. And every night, as the stars twinkled above, Henry fell asleep with a big smile, surrounded by friends who loved him.

And they all lived happily ever after.

The End

www.ingramcontent.com/pod-product-compliance
Lightning Source LLC
LaVergne TN
LVHW072335080526
838199LV00108B/383